HUNGER SHARK

EYE OF THE TIGER SHARK

EYE OF THE TIGER SHARK

By Ace Landers

Book 2

Featuring the stars of

SCHOLASTIC

Special thanks to our chums at Ubisoft and Future Games of London, and a jaw-some thanks to Sam Fry, Valentina Marchetti, Caroline Lamache, Anthony Marcantonio, Lena Barendt, Thomas Veyrat, James Varma, and Giorgia La Rocca.

ISBN 978-1-338-56872-1

10 9 8 7 6 5 4 3 2 1   20 21 22 23 24

Printed in the U.S.A. 40
First printing 2020

Book design by Mercedes Padró

ONE

The Morning Announcements

Tammy Aiko could barely contain her excitement. Today was the day she'd waited for. Today it would finally happen!

A few weeks ago, Tammy, her best friend, Kyle, and their new friend Alex had founded the Marine Science Club at Waverly Middle School. The only problem? The club wasn't exactly, well . . . *cool*. And that made Tammy sad, because marine science was pretty awesome.

The three friends, representing the Marine Science Club, had ventured to Tiburon Cove down by the beach, where they'd come across not one, but *three* wild sharks! And the sharks needed the friends' help. The smallest one, a porbeagle, had gotten trapped in some pesky plastic. Thankfully, the Marine Science Club was able to free the little guy and give him a happily ever after. Sometimes when Tammy was feeling down, she liked to imagine the shark swimming under the sea.

Unknowingly, Alex had recorded the whole event with his video camera. It was the perfect way for the Marine Science Club to get some exposure (and some cool points)—after all, what could be cooler than a club where you meet *sharks*? Tammy had initially pitched the feature to the school paper, but the paper wasn't interested. So now it was time for the morning announcements to do its thing!

The video was going to be *big*. It was going to put the Marine Science Club on the map. And although Tammy wasn't all that interested in being cool anymore, with more kids interested in the MSC, they'd be able to do good things for the oceans more easily, like plan a school-wide beach cleanup field trip. Tammy wanted kids to get involved in making sure no shark was in the porbeagle's position ever again.

But of course, that all rested on the success of the morning announcements.

Tammy tapped her left leg nervously

against the side of her desk. Sadly, she didn't share first period with Alex or Kyle (she had English class, they had Drawing and Painting), but she *was* excited to see what the rest of her classmates' reactions would be. Excitement? Intrigue? Fascination? She could just imagine answering all their questions now!

Finally, the Waverly Middle School logo appeared on the TV screen. The news anchor, an eighth grader named Carolyn Cho, was seated at the middle of a long table. Her hair was combed back and she was wearing a red pantsuit. Next to her was her co-anchor, a seventh-grade student named Leo McCormack. Confidentially, Tammy knew that Leo was only there because his mother, Ms. McCormack, was the morning announcements producer. Tammy knew that Leo would much rather be down at the football field, being gross and sweaty.

Carolyn squared her gaze with the camera.

"Goooooood morning, Waverly Middle!" Carolyn all but shouted into her mic. "Today's date is October first, and you're watching the Waverly Waves!"

Tammy braced herself. *It's all going to be okay*, she muttered under her breath.

"October has begun," Carolyn said in her pristine way of reporting the news. "Which means the Drama Club's school-wide Spookyfest is here! Be sure to stop by the club's table during lunch and buy a Spookygram. They're available all week."

Tammy wiggled in her seat. *Spookygrams*. She'd forgotten that the Drama Club sold Spookygrams. Kids gave the Drama Club two dollars, and then the Drama Club went around and sang spooky songs for the people who bought them. Last year her friend Beckah had bought her a Spookygram, and one of the members of the Drama Club followed her around all day and sang "Will You Be My Monster?"

Beckah. Tammy bristled. Beckah Cohen and Tammy used to be best friends, but ever since Beckah moved to the fancier part of town and became newspaper editor, they hadn't hung out. It made Tammy sad, but maybe drifting apart was what middle school was for. Besides, if all went well, maybe Beckah would run a feature on Tammy and the MSC. It's not like they were fighting or anything. Maybe MSC being cool was how she could win Beckah's friendship back!

"Today's lunch options in the cafeteria are mushroom risotto and shepherd's pie," Leo chimed in. "Tomorrow's are Greek salad and three-cheese grilled cheese."

Tammy liked shepherd's pie as much as the next person, but what she *really* wanted to hear was the Marine Science Club announcement. She was getting antsy!

"And now, we have a very special presentation from Waverly Middle School's own . . ." Carolyn said, but her lip quivered, as if she were about to say something funny. "Marine Science Club!"

Yes! Tammy almost screeched.

"Marine Science Club? I don't think I've heard of that one yet, Carolyn," Leo said.

"Right on! The Marine Science Club is a new organization devoted to preserving and learning about ocean life," Carolyn said. She was reading the exact notes that Tammy had given her; Tammy felt good to have her words read live to the entire school. "Its members include President Tamera Aiko, Vice President Alexander de la Cruz, and Treasurer Kyle Ray. And those three students have a real treat for us this morning . . . Leo, can you press 'Play,' please?"

"You got it," Leo said. He flipped a switch.

The screen went black. Then it fizzled out into the video recording that Alex had taken at the beach.

Tammy was instantly taken back to two weeks ago, when she, Kyle, and Alex had rescued the poor porbeagle at the beach. She heard her own voice call out, "High tide!" There was lots of splashing in the water, and the faint image of a shark. Then the clip was done.

Tammy's leg stopped bouncing. That was it. They'd done it.

The MSC has arrived, Tammy thought.

The screen went back to Carolyn and Leo. They both looked silent. Finally, Carolyn spoke.

"That was . . . something," Carolyn said.

Not missing a beat, Leo replied, "You bet. I'm not entirely sure what I just saw, but I've been told that's some exclusive footage from the Marine Science Club. Or should we say, the Photo Editing Club! They swim with *sharks*, folks!"

Tammy heard the other kids in class roar with laughter.

Photo Editing Club? She wasn't sure what that was all about—but it was most likely about Kyle. He was a great illustrator, and as long as Tammy had known him, he was always sketching something or another.

Tammy thought the clip was great. She scanned the room, waiting for her classmates to ask questions about the club (she'd even prepared a little spiel), but as she glanced around, she almost felt like the rest of her classmates were avoiding her. Was Tammy imagining things, or would they not look her way? No one's eyes met hers.

What was going on?

Finally, Tammy couldn't stay quiet anymore. She turned to the girl sitting next to her, Miranda Quinones.

"Everything okay?" Tammy asked.

Miranda shot a look at her.

"Um," Miranda said. "I guess. *I'm* okay. But what's with the, uh . . ." Miranda lowered her voice. "Fake sharks?"

TWO

A Shark-tastrophe

Fake sharks?!

Tammy wanted to scream.

The video was not fake! The sharks were not fake! The Marine Science Club was not a fraud!

Tammy had really seen a hammerhead, a porbeagle, and a mako shark out in the wild. And Kyle and Alex had seen them too. And they were even kind of friends with them!

Tammy opened her mouth to say something, but just as she did so, her English teacher, Ms. Kapoor, silenced the room.

"Did everyone do last night's reading?" Ms. Kapoor asked. Then class time began.

But Tammy couldn't focus on *Moby Dick*. She was too wrapped up in what had happened. People didn't believe that the MSC had befriended some sharks. Even when they had irrefutable evidence. Tammy could feel her eyes beginning to water.

Tammy grabbed the bathroom pass and made a beeline toward the bathroom. Once there, she flung herself into the stall and began to sob. It wasn't fair. Not fair, not fair, not *fair*! She'd done everything right. Why had this happened?

Tammy wadded some toilet paper up and

dried her eyes. She was about to leave when she heard someone with a familiar voice walk into the bathroom and stop at the mirror. Tammy recognized that voice instantly—it was Beckah Cohen. And through the crack of the stall, Tammy could see that Beckah was speaking to a redheaded girl Tammy didn't know.

"You know, I told her we can't print anything without cold, hard evidence," Beckah said. "It's not my fault that the morning announcements don't screen what they air. I mean, it's so sad, isn't it? Imagine being *so* desperate for friends that you have to resort to a fake science club. Really!"

Tammy's heart sank.

Beckah had to be talking about her—about the Marine Science Club. And Beckah seemed to think that on top of it *all*, she was "desperate for friends."

This was it. This was the worst thing that could have possibly happened.

Tammy felt like a puddle of mush.

Tammy tried to make herself as small as possible in the stall. She didn't want Beckah and the redheaded girl to see her legs in the gap between the door and the floor. She took deep breaths. Then, when the coast was clear and the girls had left, she slipped back into English class, feeling a hundred—no, a thousand—times worse than she had before.

•

At lunch, Tammy sat with Kyle and Alex.

"This is a shark-tastrophe," Tammy said. She didn't even touch the shepherd's pie in front of her.

Kyle was busy drawing his Interesting Thing of the day. Each day, he picked one thing, and one thing only, to draw. By the end of the day, he'd be an expert on it. Today, that thing seemed to be a portrait of Carolyn Cho on the morning announcements.

Alex, however, had no such appetite problem. He dug into his mashed potatoes and got a glob on his pants.

"Well, *we* know we're not lying," Alex said. "Besides, wasn't the whole point to save the sharks? And we did that. So we still win."

Tammy wanted to knock some sense into her friend.

"But now our club is *ruined*!" she nearly spat. "How will anyone want to help the sharks when they don't even believe the sharks are real?"

Kyle raised an eyebrow.

"Tammy," he said, putting his colored pencil down. "How many years have we been best friends?"

"Twelve," Tammy replied. "Ever since we were a year old."

"And do you know how many times I've seen you give up on something you're passionate about?" Kyle asked.

Tammy shook her head.

"Zero," Kyle said. "Zero times. That's very special, T. And you *cannot* give up now."

Alex put his arm around Tammy.

"You know what we gotta do, right?" Alex asked.

Tammy knew but she didn't want to say it.

"Clear our heads," said Kyle. "And the best way to do that . . . is to go back to the beach."

THREE

It's Hammerhead Time

That very same moment, the ocean was calm. Almost *too* calm, actually. It was a perfect condition for Hammerhead's newest experiment. The medium-sized shark was a skilled inventor. And today, she had a new goal.

Hammerhead swam to the top of her sunken pirate ship with a net in her mouth. The ship was Hammerhead's special place, a place where she kept her collection of man-made treasures. But the ship was more than just a storage space. It was also a place where Hammerhead was *free* to invent anything she dreamed of. Where there were no judging eyes or anyone telling her what to do.

Today, Hammerhead wanted to *fly*.

As a shark, Hammerhead had skimmed the surface of the water before. She'd even caught air a few times. But Hammerhead wanted to soar like the fluffy things that flapped across the deep sky above the ocean. The things humans called birds.

Hammerhead knew that sharks couldn't fly. Not naturally, anyway. But there were no laws of nature that said she couldn't *invent* something!

Hammerhead swam back and forth

between the ship's old and worn masts, looping the net she carried until it was so tight that the strings vibrated when they were plucked. She'd gotten the idea from watching a human playing in the deep ocean. There was a contraption that the human used to bounce on, and every time they bounced on it, their little human body went higher and higher. Hammerhead called it a Stomperine, because the more you stomped, the higher you jumped.

There was only one problem. Sharks don't stomp. However, they *can* swim really fast. Thanks to a stopwatch that Hammerhead had found underwater, she clocked her fastest swimming at twenty-five miles per hour. Not bad for a shark with a head named after a clunky human tool.

All she needed now was a Stomperine of her own. That's where the net came into play. Hammerhead had borrowed a net from some nice fishermen who kept throwing it into the water. After seeing them throw it a few times, Hammerhead realized that perhaps the fishermen were trying to get rid of the net. Not to mention that all the fish near it kept getting tangled up and trapped. So Hammerhead stuck her head out of the water and asked nicely if she could have their net. The fishermen screamed and drove their boat away, which Hammerhead assumed was human for, "Yes, be our guest and please take our net."

So she did.

With the net tied tightly, Hammerhead swam far away from the sunken pirate ship. She had measured out the exact distance she needed to travel so that she would hit her top speed just as she bounced on the Stomperine, which would blast her up, up, and way above the water.

She reached the teeth marks she had etched on the side of a giant clam and took a few deep breaths. Hammerhead knew she wouldn't be able to breathe above water, so she would have to time her last gasp just right. When she was ready, Hammerhead bolted forward, leaving a trail of bubbles in her wake.

•

After school, Tammy, Kyle, and Alex walked along the boardwalk at the beach. They didn't really have any set plans—they just wanted to get their minds off the unfortunate events of the day.

"I just read a really cool comic book," Alex

said, trying to change the topic from the shark-tastrophe to something more . . . positive. "It's about a dragon slayer who is secretly a dragon but only his cat knows."

"That's cool," Tammy replied, though she was super monotone. It didn't sound like she was paying attention to Alex at all.

Just then, there was a loud noise. It sounded like someone yelling, *"Heyyyyy-yo!"*

"Tammy, watch out!" Kyle called out. Tammy saw a ball flying right at her and jumped underneath a bench for cover. *Crash!* The football landed right where she had been standing.

"Jeez," Tammy muttered, wiping off the sand on her knees. "Who *was* that?"

A tall, muscular kid ran over.

At first, Tammy only saw his shadow. But

even the shadow was enough to know who it was. Only one person in their whole town was as big and strong as that shadow. And that person was Leo McCormack.

"Leo," Tammy whispered.

Leo McCormack grabbed the ball.

"Aw, man," he said, inspecting it. "Some air's gotten out. Hey, I didn't hit you, did I?" he asked Tammy.

"No," Tammy grumbled. *Though you pretty much hit me emotionally, this morning,* she wanted to say.

Leo helped her up. Then he took a good, long look at Tammy, as if trying to place where he knew her from.

"Oy! You go to Waverly Middle, don't you?" he asked.

Tammy nodded.

"So what brings you to the beach today?"

"I'm a member of the Marine Science Club," Tammy said, in the most powerful voice she could muster. "We come to the beach to clear our heads. And to—"

Leo cocked an eyebrow.

"Meet with sharks?"

"Yeah. Exactly," Tammy replied.

Tammy could feel her face flush. In all her years of knowing Leo McCormack at school, Tammy wasn't sure she had ever really spoken to him. Their moms had been friendly over the years—Mrs. Aiko sometimes volunteered at the school, and Ms. McCormack worked there—but Leo was usually busy playing some form of sport, and Tammy, well, wasn't. While she'd like to pretend that getting trapped by seaweed was something rare for her, it happened quite often. Tammy could trip over her own shoelaces if she didn't remember to tie them!

Tammy had heard some stories about Leo, though, and she always thought he was kind of a bully. He did things like throw basketballs and footballs all over the place. Plus, he was pretty mean on the morning announcements.

Out of everyone in the world, why did Leo McCormack *have to throw the ball at me?* Tammy thought.

"You know that people don't really *meet with sharks*, right?" Leo asked.

Tammy harrumphed.

"Well, *we* did," she replied. "So if you don't want to believe us, there's nothing else I can really say to you. We have more important things to do. Like—"

Tammy was about to say "like save the ocean," but before she could do that, a white seagull circled around them. It dipped low, then landed directly on the football.

"What the?" Leo said.

The seagull had something inside its mouth. And it wasn't just *any* something. It was a purple ribbon—Tammy's biodegradable purple ribbon, the very same one that her grandfather had given her one summer, and the very same one that she'd gifted to the hammerhead shark only a few weeks ago.

Tammy's eyes widened.

Hammerhead's calling to us!

FOUR
Back to the Beach

Hammerhead loved speed swimming. The ocean blurred around her as she focused on her target. The white net stood at the ready. Hammerhead felt the swift drift of the water ripple all around her as she moved faster and faster. She braced for her bouncy impact just as another shark swam into view.

That shark was Hammerhead's good friend Porbeagle. And Porbeagle was chomping on

his squeaker toy—*squeak, squeak!*—while float-
ing in the worst place possible: right in front of
Hammerhead's Stomperine!

Hammerhead pulled up at the last minute,
narrowly avoiding Porbeagle, but also narrowly avoiding the net too! She was moving
so fast now, Hammerhead was worried she
might spin out of control and crash into
another sea creature like Tiger Shark. And
Hammerhead *really* didn't want to do that.

But then a funny thing happened.
Hammerhead began to slow down.

Hammerhead looked behind her. Although
Hammerhead's body had missed the
net, Hammerhead's *tail* did not miss the net.
In fact, Hammerhead's tail had caught the
net, which meant the net had now caught
Hammerhead!

Hmm, maybe this was a good thing, Hammerhead thought. She had wanted to use the bouncy Stomperine to fly, but the Stomperine had turned into a slingshot.

Whoosh!

Before Hammerhead could finish her thought, the net snapped back into place, pulling her with it and tossing her hard in the other direction. Hammerhead waved to Porbeagle as she passed the small shark in the opposite direction, then she braced for the worst.

Thud! Hammerhead bumped into a different shark, and they went tumbling into a slow-waving forest of seaweed.

Why can't my plans ever go right? Hammerhead thought.

The shark she hit had a wide, crooked smile

and two eyes that were full of excitement. It was Mako, another of Hammerhead's best friends, and Mako had more energy than usual.

Mako held a balled-up piece of soggy trash in his mouth. And with a throaty *gaw*, he coughed and spit it onto Hammerhead.

Yuck! thought Hammerhead. *Mako! We talked about this!* Then with her fins she unraveled the trash.

It was written in human language, but Hammerhead knew an adventure when she saw one. She recognized the pictures on the paper. They were all things to find at the beach! This was a scavenger hunt! Better yet, this was a *sign*. The humans she had met last time must be back—and they'd sent a letter to her!

Hammerhead knew what had to be done.

It was time to go back to the beach!

Hammerhead, Porbeagle, and Mako rushed to Tiburon Cove, the spot where they had met the kids before. This time Hammerhead kept a close eye on Porbeagle. The last time they'd visited the cove, Porbeagle had wandered off and caused a lot of trouble, but that was also how the sharks and humans had become friends.

When they arrived, Hammerhead popped her head eagerly out of the water first. She scanned around excitedly. But there was no one in sight. The cove was completely empty—except for one of those fluffy flying things.

A seagull! Mako seemed to say.

Hammerhead cast a glance at the seagull. Then she got an idea!

With Mako's help, they unraveled the purple biodegradable ribbon that Hammerhead had tied comfortably around her fin.

Porbeagle, who was somewhat of an artist, collected rocks and made a picture of Tammy with them. Then the sharks approached the seagull.

Hey, bird, Hammerhead seemed to say. *Can you take this to our friend? She might be elsewhere on the beach.*

Hammerhead dropped the ribbon in front of the bird.

The seagull stared for a moment. Then it cawed.

I think it wants something as a trade, Hammerhead thought.

Mako knew just what to do!

He dove deep beneath the ocean and

grabbed a large, slimy fish. Then he dropped it at the seagull's feet.

The seagull stared at the fish for a moment. Seagulls *love* fish, almost as much as sharks do! It bobbed its head as if nodding, scooped up the fish, ate it, and flew off with the ribbon.

I really hope it finds Tammy, Hammerhead thought.

FIVE

A Message from a Bird

"You can't be serious," said Leo McCormack. "Nope. Nuh-uh. No way. A *shark* cannot be summoning a *human* to Tiburon Cove."

Leo, Tammy, Kyle, and Alex were huddled in a circle on the boardwalk. The seagull had dropped the ribbon at Tammy's feet and then flown away. Tammy now held the ribbon with her left hand. She kept turning it over, wondering too if this was all real.

"You just saw a seagull drop Tammy's purple ribbon at her feet, and you're questioning if we're friends with sharks?" Alex quipped.

Leo laughed.

"Of course, I'm questioning it!" he said. "I mean, no offense, but how do you even know that's Tammy's ribbon? There's lots of trash on this beach. Maybe the seagull just picked it up."

"No, it's definitely my ribbon," Tammy said. She fished her phone out of her pocket and jabbed it at him. Her phone screensaver was a photo of her and her grandfather. Tammy was wearing the ribbon.

"That still doesn't prove anything," Leo said. "There must be thousands of purple ribbons in the world."

The thought of seeing the sharks again

energized Tammy. All she wanted to do was jump up and venture to Tiburon Cove, where they'd met with the sharks before.

"Look, we don't have time to argue with you," Tammy said. "It's low tide now, so if we don't head out to the cove to meet our friends, we'll miss them."

Tammy started to stride away. Alex followed her. But Kyle stayed behind for just a moment with Leo.

Kyle wasn't particularly loud. He was a good illustrator, and he'd saved Porbeagle and agreed to be the Marine Science Club's treasurer. And he was Tammy's best friend. But Kyle was also a good leader. Sometimes he knew just what to say.

"I know you don't believe us, Leo," Kyle said. "And that's fine. No loss. But consider this. What if we *are* telling the truth?"

Leo thought about it. And then, to even Leo's surprise, he picked up his football and followed the other three to Tiburon Cove.

•

Hammerhead, Mako, and Porbeagle waited at the cove. Hammerhead was starting to get impatient. *What if the seagull didn't find Tammy? What if it didn't even try?*

Porbeagle tried to calm Hammerhead down. *Let's play a game!*

Porbeagle grabbed a conch shell in his mouth and tossed it. *Zoom!* Mako darted after it. Then he tried throwing it toward Hammerhead, but Hammerhead didn't budge.

Hammerhead would have loved to go on a scavenger hunt with the humans. She felt stupid. What if they got the invite too late? What if the invite wasn't even from them? What if—and Hammerhead *really* hoped not—something had happened to them?

Cheer up, Hams, Porbeagle seemed to say. *We can have lots more fun in the ocean.*

Yeah! Weren't you inventing something, anyway? Mako seemed to say back.

Hammerhead shook her head from side to side. She was so disappointed.

Finally, Hammerhead decided it was time to go back in the water. Maybe if Hammerhead learned to fly like the seagull, she could have found the humans instead! All the more reason for Hammerhead's invention to come to life . . .

Just as the sharks were about to descend into the deep, Hammerhead heard a noise. She perked up. Could it be?

Squawk! Squawk! The same seagull flew in. It dropped low and perched on a nearby rock. It faced the opening of the cove. If Hammerhead squinted just right, she could make out three shadows.

Three?

Wait. No. *Four!*

"The sharks!" a voice called out. "I knew it! I knew they'd be back!"

Hammerhead, Mako, and Porbeagle splashed around.

The humans! They had finally come!

SIX

A Shark-tastic Reunion

Tammy saw the sharks first: Mako, his head poking up; Porbeagle, splashing along; and, although she didn't like to admit it, Hammerhead, her favorite—a beautiful gray shark with an unusually shaped head.

"They're here! They're really here!" Tammy called. She could almost dance, she was so happy! It had been a few weeks since they'd last encountered the sharks, and she was

43

beginning to think they wouldn't see them again.

"Porby!" Kyle called. He dashed right up to where his favorite, Porbeagle, was, and immediately started patting him on the head. Kyle and Porbeagle had bonded before—after all, it was Kyle who had saved the little shark when he had gotten stuck.

Alex and the mako shark greeted each other with eagerness. They were something of a pair too—the cheerleaders, in a sense, of their own respective teams.

And when Tammy and Hammerhead saw each other, they both melted. Tammy never felt quite as at home as she did when she was with Hammerhead. They seemed just to *get* each other in a way she couldn't quite express.

"Oh, we missed you so *much*," Tammy said,

scratching Hammerhead gently between her eyes. "I'm glad to see that you're all okay. We got your message. Here's your ribbon back. I think it's now more yours than it ever was mine." Tammy handed her purple ribbon back to Hammerhead, who graciously accepted it.

Hammerhead emitted a few bubbles for Tammy. Tammy knew that meant *I missed you too*.

But just when the reunion had started, Hammerhead got distracted. Her eyes darted right behind Tammy to where another shadow was. Tammy followed Hammerhead's gaze.

"Don't be frightened," Tammy said. "That's Leo McCormack. He's not going to hurt you. In fact, he didn't even believe you existed."

Tammy tossed her long, black hair over

her shoulder and turned around to face Leo.

"Well, what are you waiting for?" she said, smiling bigger now than she had all day. "You're here, aren't you? Come say hi!"

Leo laughed nervously.

"Um," he said. It was clear that Leo was *very* uncomfortable. "Are you sure those aren't, er, puppets? Maybe a new kind of Spookygram the Drama Club is putting on?"

Tammy made a face.

"Oh, is big, tough Waverly Middle School quarterback star Leo McCormack afraid of a tiny, little shark? Come say hi! Or—oh! I think the *shark* wants to say hi to *you*!"

Hammerhead zoomed right up to Leo, who was at the edge of the water, and did a flip in the water. Hammerhead cast a look back at Tammy, as if to say, *this is fun!*

Leo had no choice. Tammy had said the magic words, and Hammerhead was so gosh darn adorable. He bent down and stuck his hand out slowly. Hammerhead jumped right up to it as if giving him a high five.

"I—I can't believe it," Leo stuttered. "This can't be real."

"Of course it's real," replied Tammy. "It's what I've been telling you. What I've been telling all of Waverly Middle School. Sharks are *friendly*. They just want us to stop polluting the oceans. They want to live among us really happily. And *that's* one of the reasons why marine science is super, super cool." Now Tammy turned to Hammerhead. "Alright, girl. Is there something you want to show me?"

Hammerhead took out the scavenger hunt paper that Mako had found. She finned it over to Tammy, who held it in her hands.

Tammy looked at the scavenger hunt sadly. Then she looked back at Hammerhead.

"This isn't from us," Tammy said. "I'm so sorry."

The paper made Tammy feel bad. Giving Hammerhead a biodegradable purple ribbon was one thing. It would never harm the sharks because it would disintegrate with enough time under water. Plus, it was made from recyclable materials. But the paper wasn't. It was somebody's trash that they'd left behind. And that was exactly how poor Porbeagle had ended up in the plastic two weeks ago.

"Pollution is harming the ocean," Tammy told Leo. "And the sharks need our help. The sharks *need* us. We were hoping to get some more kids at Waverly on board . . ."

Leo shook his head.

"Alright," he said. "Say no more. I understand."

At this, Alex perked up.

"So you'll tell everyone we're not frauds?"

"Yeah, you owe us," said Kyle.

Leo shrugged his shoulders.

"Honestly, I only say things on the morning announcements that are given to me. I don't make up anything on my own," he replied. "I'm sorry for the hurt I caused. Really sorry. But I believe you now. So I think . . . maybe, if you run an event, or do something else, we can run another ad for you guys. And there'll be no photo editing jokes. That, I promise."

Tammy was thrilled.

"That's great," she said. "Because the MSC has some ideas."

SEVEN
S.W.B.C.F.T.

The next day at school, Tammy, Kyle, and Alex sat in Mr. Lopez's science class for a meeting of the Marine Science Club.

"So I was thinking about our next great plan for the beach cleanup field trip. There's clearly lots of pollution still on the beach, and Leo's promised to help," Tammy said. "But the trip needs a name. And if I'm being honest, 'School-Wide Beach Cleanup Field Trip' is kind of a mouthful."

"But that's exactly what it is!" Alex said. "Maybe we can call it the S.W.B.C.F.T."

"Swibcuffed," Kyle replied, pronouncing all the letters in Alex's acronym.

The three friends laughed. That was *not* going to be the beach trip name.

Tammy wrote three ideas on the whiteboard. So far, she had:

Beach Beach Baby

Beachin' It with the MSC

Beach Day!

None of them were quite right.

"'How about 'Surf's Up, Science Buffs'?" suggested Alex.

Tammy and Kyle exchanged looks. Alex was new to Waverly Middle; he didn't know the kids yet. But Tammy and Kyle could hardly imagine everyone at Waverly Middle reacting positively to being called science buffs. Especially not after the shark-tastrophe fiasco.

"I like 'Surf's Up,'" Tammy said, trying to be as diplomatic as possible. (After all, she was the Marine Science Club's president.) "I'll add that to the list."

Tammy wrote it right under "Beach Day!" There wasn't really anything wrong with "Beach Day!" but it just seemed too . . . on the nose. Which was in a way what they needed . . . and in a way, totally *not*.

"I think we need something straightforward and to the point," Tammy said. "Kind of like 'Marine Science Club.'"

"Ooh, how about 'Marine Science Presents'?" Alex suggested. "We can call this

'Marine Science Presents: Beach Day!,' then if we do more field trips, it can be things like 'Marine Science Presents: Museum Day!,' and so on and so forth."

Tammy's face lit up. That was perfect!

"I love it!" she squealed.

"Nice job," Kyle told Alex.

Tammy erased the other names on the board and wrote "Marine Science Presents" in big, blocky letters. Then she dug out her phone and texted Leo. It was time for the morning announcements, take two!

•

The next day, Tammy was prepared for the morning announcements. She'd sent Leo a script that she'd carefully crafted, and he promised that he, not Carolyn, would deliver the news.

The only thing left, now, was to wait.

The morning announcements logo went up on-screen and Tammy sat back, ready to watch.

"Goooooood morning, Waverly Middle!" Carolyn said. "Today's date is October third, and you're watching the Waverly Waves!"

The morning announcements theme music played.

"Today's lunch options in the cafeteria include chicken and waffles and tomato bisque soup," Carolyn continued. "Tomorrow's options are chicken fingers and vegetarian fried rice."

Now the screen panned to Leo. Tammy braced herself. She knew this was the moment.

"Spookygrams are still on sale through the end of the week from the Drama Club," Leo said. "In more club news, the Marine Science

Club is pleased to announce their first annual event: Marine Science Presents: Beach Day!"

Tammy scanned her eyes across the room. At the mention of "Marine Science Club," she could tell that the rest of her classmates were at the very least interested, if only to poke fun at her.

"Marine Science Club? That still exists?" Carolyn laughed into her mic.

"Oh yes, it does!" said Leo. "The Marine Science Club is proud to host Marine Science Club Presents: Beach Day!, a day in which all the kids at Waverly Middle School are invited to help clean up the beach. Cleaning up the beach is important because it ensures that wildlife won't get harmed by litter. Tickets cost five dollars, and the beach day takes place during school. Waivers are needed and must be signed by a parent or guardian."

Tammy had to admit it. Leo was *good* at being clear, concise, and delivering effectively. Even if his main thing was sports, he wasn't half-bad at the morning announcements!

"The beach day takes place next week," Leo continued. "Submit your waivers and cash to their treasurer, Kyle Ray. And remember to bring sunscreen!"

Carolyn was a pro at giving the people what they want.

"But will you see any sharks?" she said and smirked.

"I guess you'll have to go and find out," Leo said.

•

Tammy, Kyle, and Alex got special permission from their teachers to leave for lunch ten minutes early. They scooted a table into the cafeteria, right by the register, and set up a display. Kyle rolled out a paper banner that said "Marine Science Presents: Beach Day! Sign-Ups" on it, with his own signature logo and a drawing of a porbeagle shark. Alex had a collection of field trip waivers at his station. And Tammy had a sign-up sheet. The five dollars they collected from each student would ensure that everyone got lunch on the field trip, which Alex's parents—who owned a pizza shop at the beach—had graciously agreed to provide.

"That announcement was really great this morning," Alex said, making conversation. "I guess it's nice to have Leo McCormack in our Mc-*corner*!" He laughed.

Kyle laughed too, but Tammy kept a straight face.

"He is responsible for making us a laugh-ingstock at first, so he's not totally forgiven," she said. "But I'm hoping we have a good turn-out. I guess we'll just have to wait and see!"

Bring! Bring! Briiiiing! The lunch bell sounded. Tammy noticed her leg was tapping again.

A few kids walked into the cafeteria, jumped into the food line, and then took their seats. Some of them cast sidelong looks at the MSC table. Tammy saw a few kids get up with dollar bills in their hands, but then they walked over to the Drama Club's booth.

Oh no, Tammy thought. *This is going to be another disaster!*

But then Alex prodded Tammy on the arm and said, "Look!" Two girls were getting out of their seats and making their way toward the table. One girl was tall and redheaded, and the other girl had curly brown hair and tan skin. Tammy recognized them immediately. It was Beckah and the girl from the bathroom!

Beckah and the girl approached the table.

"Tammy, Kyle," Beckah said, smiling big. "It's so nice to see you."

Tammy grimaced. "Hi, Beckah," she said.

"Congratulations on the beach cleanup, friends," Beckah said. "That's a big undertaking you have there. It's five dollars each, right? Here's a ten—Carina and I are very interested in going."

Alex took their money. Then he handed them two waivers.

"I'm Alex, by the way," he said.

Beckah gave Alex a once-over, from his

eager face to his death metal band T-shirt.

"Pleasure," Beckah said, even though it was clear that it wasn't.

"See you on the trip," Carina said. "Bye now!"

Then they left.

After Beckah and Carina, there was a stream of other kids. Meg Levitz and Connor Jenkins came up; Steven Agarwal and Norah Giron. Even some of the eighth graders, led by Carolyn Cho, stopped by. Tammy couldn't contain herself. It was basically the entire school!

"As much as they seem to hate the Marine Science Club, they seem to love beach field trips," Alex said, bemused.

"This is going to be the best field trip ever!" Tammy exclaimed.

EIGHT
Tiger Shark

After all the waivers and cash were collected, it was time to plan. Over the weekend, the three MSC members met. They pre-ordered enough pizza slices from Alex's parents for the kids, and found some biodegradable trash bags to pick up debris. Then Kyle had the brilliant idea of *also* holding a contest. The kid who picked up the most trash would win a gift card to the pizza shop!

On Alex's side of things, he worked with his parents to make sure they weren't creating a lot of waste. He was adamant that they not use any plastic straws, not just for the beach day but for *any* day.

"Did you know that plastic straws are the eleventh most-littered item in the ocean?" Alex told anyone who would listen. "And they take up to two hundred years to decompose. That's *two* whole lifetimes!"

Tammy had even taken it upon herself to go down to Tiburon Cove over the weekend. She hadn't seen the sharks, but she did see the same seagull as before.

"If you see my friends, can you tell them about our beach cleanup?" she asked. If the sharks visited, and showed everyone how friendly they were . . . that would mean a lot for the MSC!

The plan was in motion. And soon, the day of the field trip came.

•

Hammerhead was working on her flying suit when Mako swam over to her.

I think the seagull wants to tell you something, Mako bubbled.

The seagull? From before? Hammerhead's spirits lifted! If it was the seagull, maybe it was a message from the humans!

Hammerhead and Mako went zooming through the water, eager to meet the seagull at Tiburon Cove.

A playful eel squiggled past Mako and bristled with electricity. Before anyone could say "shocking shark," Mako took off after the eel. He chased it and tried to chomp it, but every time he caught the eel, a sharp snap of electricity surged through him. Hammerhead shook with laughter as Mako turned himself into a shark X-ray over and over again with each shock. *ZAP! SNAP! ZIZZ! ZOW!*

Finally, the eel zipped away, leaving Mako energized but happy. As he swam back over to Hammerhead, Mako crackled with massive volts of eel electricity.

Hammerhead smiled. She loved her ridiculous friend. Shark life would be pretty boring without Mako—and without Porbeagle, of course.

Speaking of Porbeagle, they found him basking in some coral. He saw his friends and flopped over, eager and ready to join on their new expedition.

As they continued swimming, a rush of bubbles blew by them. Porbeagle's tongue hung out of his mouth as he happily chomped at the bubbles, but Hammerhead had a bad feeling about this. She'd seen these bubbles before. They came from the wake of a bigger shark. A faster shark. The kind of shark that she had wanted to *avoid*.

Then a large orange shark darted out of the trench. He stopped in front of Hammerhead and flexed his muscles, showing off to the others. Hammerhead groaned.

It was Tiger Shark.

Hello, friends, Tiger Shark breathed. *What are we doing today?*

We're just enjoying ourselves, Hammerhead communicated back. *Don't mind us.*

Hammerhead tried to keep on her way, but

Tiger decided to follow. He coughed up a fish bone and used it as a comb, running it over his gills. Hammerhead had to admit that this move made him look cool, but she was not going to clap for him. He wasn't the center of attention.

She swam around him again, then felt a tap on her shoulder. With a deep breath, she turned around ready to scream at him, but Tiger was too interested.

I have nothing to do. I want to join you, Tiger motioned back.

Well, you can't. We have a secret club, said Hammerhead.

A secret club?

Now Porbeagle started bounding around excitedly.

It's called the Terrestrial Science Club. We meet with humans above the sea!

Hammerhead almost wished she had a video camera to record Tiger's reaction.

Tiger at first thought they were joking. He even pretended to laugh. He smiled at them, showing his big, toothy grin. But when he realized they weren't joking, his amusement quickly turned to horror. *Humans?* Tiger seemed to say. *Humans?*

In the shark world, humans are just as scary as sharks are to humans. Humans pollute the ocean, and they fish the sharks, and they fish the fish that the sharks eat, making them have less food. Not to mention, they had big, scary boat-things. Tiger didn't like boat-things. No shark did.

Well, now I have to go with you! Tiger motioned back. *If I don't, who is going to protect you three?*

Tiger flashed another deathly smile, showing off all his chomping teeth.

Hammerhead wanted to protest, but before she opened her jaw, she saw something gray and graceful flittering above the water. It was the seagull!

Hammerhead and the other three sharks poked their heads up. The seagull gave them great news: The kids were coming back! And they were bringing a whole bunch of other kids too!

Tiger couldn't believe what he was hearing. The beach was going to be flooded with measly, unruly, ungrateful *humans*? And Hammerhead, Mako, and Porbeagle didn't even care?

Consider me the fourth member of the Terrestrial Science Club, Tiger motioned back.

Tiger may have been the biggest, meanest shark in the sea, but he cared about his friends deeply. He didn't want them getting hurt. *I'm going on this beach trip if it's the last thing I do*, thought Tiger.

NINE
Beach Day

Hammerhead really, really, really wished that Tiger hadn't joined her friends. It's not that Hammerhead didn't like Tiger (Tiger definitely had his good days), Hammerhead just didn't want him disrupting the flow of things. Especially not when their interactions with the humans were so good. But now that he knew about the humans' Beach Day! plan,

Hammerhead knew there was no way to shake him off.

We'll just have to make sure he doesn't bite anyone, Hammerhead thought. *Or scare anyone. 'Cuz that would be*—Hammerhead gulped—*bad*.

On the day of the beach trip, Hammerhead glanced at her reflection in the mirror on her pirate ship. She wanted to make sure she looked nice and spiffy and totally *not* scary. Which is probably not hard for a human to do—but *beyond* hard for a shark!

With Mako and Porbeagle's help, Hammerhead tied Tammy's ribbon into a bow. Then they used a comb to put it on top of Hammerhead's head, right between her two eyes. Hammerhead felt a little silly, but even Porbeagle said she looked nice!

When they were ready, the three sharks went to Tiburon Cove together. And of course, Tiger followed.

They're really your friends? Tiger bubbled.

Aye, Mako responded.

Tiger shrugged. He promised that if the humans played nice, then he would too. But Hammerhead wasn't sure if that's what Tiger really thought. She was skeptical, to say the least.

Meanwhile, Tammy, Alex, and Kyle were at the beach. They announced the contest to everyone: The kid who cleaned up the most litter would win a gift card to the pizzeria!

Wahoo! Hooray! Yippee! the kids cheered.

I guess that's the answer to everything, Tammy thought. *Field trips where you miss school . . . and get pizza.*

The three MSC members passed out bags for everyone to collect trash. And then they were on their way.

On the boardwalk, Tammy found a lot of gross stuff. She picked up Italian ice cream cups, discarded sunscreen bottles, and even some plastic containers from the burrito shop a mile away.

Alex collected some things too. He and Kyle shared a bag, and together they found tons of water bottles, unused Band-Aids, and gum wrappers.

"Any of this stuff could have trapped Porbeagle," Alex said sadly, glancing down at his pile. "I'm glad that now it won't."

Tammy agreed. She wondered what her grandfather would think. He was a marine biologist in Japan, and he was the person who got her interested in the field to begin with. When Tammy grew up, she wanted to be just like him.

Tammy walked down the beach, eager to see what everyone else had collected. She found Miranda Quinones down by the shore.

"Any luck?" Tammy asked Miranda.

Miranda made a face.

"I found a candy wrapper," she said, pointing to a sole candy wrapper inside her bag. "Pretty gross, yeah?"

"*Super* gross," Tammy said. Then she flashed a smile at her. "Thanks for nabbing it!"

Annabel Magno had a huge collection of soda cans in her bag. Ashton Amarado had even more. So did Bex Kubila and Justin Harmond. The more Tammy walked, the more kids she saw collecting trash. The kids at

Waverly Middle School were giving back. They were doing something. Tammy felt amazing!

She almost wasn't even bothered by the group of kids gathered on the beach who were *not* picking up trash. It seemed like those kids, a group of ten or so, had decided the beach trip was more about suntanning and having fun. They even had a volleyball out.

Almost not bothered.

That's completely awful, Tammy thought. *Who would even do such a thing?*

Tammy knew just what she had to do. She waltzed over to their camp. And when she got there, she recognized Leo McCormack instantly. His big, hulking figure could be picked out in a crowd anywhere.

"Leo!" Tammy called. "You're not helping out?"

Leo was wearing a pair of giant sunglasses. He saw Tammy and tried to ignore her. But Tammy was not very good at being ignored.

"Leo McCormack!" Tammy screeched. She screeched so loud that all of Leo's friends turned and looked. Tammy gulped. Two of Leo's friends were Beckah and the redheaded girl, Carina.

Beckah's sunk this low too? Tammy thought.

Leo faced Tammy, held up a soda, and shrugged.

"A beach day is a beach day," he said nonchalantly.

Tammy could feel her face hot and red, and she didn't think it was because of her sunburn.

"You, out of everybody here, should be helping us clean the beach," Tammy said, loud enough so that everyone could listen. "After all, you've *seen* the sharks!"

The other kids stopped what they were doing. They all looked at Leo.

"You've seen the sharks?" Beckah repeated. Her gaze kept darting back and forth between Leo and Tammy. "Leo, what is this nonsense?"

Leo took a deep sigh.

"I mean, I—" He took a glance at Tammy. "Yeah. I've seen the sharks."

There was a collective *oomf.*

"Oh my gosh," Beckah muttered quickly. "Everyone, *Leo* is in on this too! The marine science hogwash!" The other kids started giggling.

"No, I've really seen the sharks," Leo replied. "I'm not a liar."

Beckah continued laughing. The horde of other kids laughed too. One of them even called him Lion Shark.

"Leo, Leo, fins on fire," chanted a boy with slick brown hair.

"Dudes, stop teasing," said Leo. "You don't believe me? Fine. I'll *prove* it." There was a collective gasp. "Follow me. We're going to Tiburon Cove."

TEN

A Leo, a Tiger, a Tammy, Oh My!

Tammy, along with other kids including Carina, Beckah, and Leo, all entered Tiburon Cove. Immediately, the kids started complaining. "It smells like rotten eggs!" Carina called out. "This place stinks worse than Principal Sutker's socks!" called another. "Ew, ew, *ew!*"

Tammy didn't like the idea of bringing

everyone to meet the sharks—she wanted their interaction to be far more organic, and ideally with people she knew would be respectful—but she was also tired of being labeled a fraud. Now was her chance to prove that she wasn't.

"You get used to it," she told them. "Now, *shush*. Be patient. They'll be here. There's three of them—a hammerhead, a mako, and a porbeagle shark."

They waited for a few minutes but nothing happened.

"I'm outta here," said Carina. "My nose can't take it anymore. I think it's going to fall off because it smells so bad in here."

"That's because Leo farted!" said another kid, someone Tammy recognized named

Reina Gaboor. Tammy did not think very highly of Reina.

Suddenly, there was bubbling coming up from the ocean. Tammy braced herself. This was it! This was Hammerhead, come to prove to everyone that they were wrong about the MSC!

"Hammerhead!" Tammy called out, running toward the bubbling. She crossed her fingers, hoping that she wouldn't trip. Thankfully, she didn't. She was right beside the bubbling, gazing out, when her heart sank.

The fin that poked out of the water was not Hammerhead's fin.

Nor was it Mako's.

Nor was it Porbeagle's.

No, this was another shark's fin.

"That's a tiger shark!" came a voice. Alex had joined the group. "Everyone, stay back!"

Of course, the kids did the opposite of listen.

"Oh, it's so *cute*," Beckah said. "Can we go see it? I want to take a selfie with her, that'll look so good in the paper—"

"No. No. NO!" shouted Tammy. "I don't know that shark. I've never seen it before. It might be dangerous. In fact, it's probably dangerous. NO ONE go near him."

Carina pretended she couldn't hear her.

"Becks, can you pass me your phone? I put it in your backpack. I need to snap this."

Tammy exchanged a helpless look with Alex, as if to say, *I need you.* Thankfully, Alex came to her call.

"Tiger sharks eat everything, from fish

to birds to squid to seals to turtles to even other sharks," Alex told everyone. "We gotta go. *Now.*"

Beckah squared her eyes on Leo. "Leo, you said you met these sharks, right? Well, now's your chance to prove it. Reach out and pet him."

"*Stop!*" Tammy yelled, but it was too late.

Leo stuck his hand out toward the tiger shark. It swam instinctively toward him, bared its teeth, and then . . . *wham!*

Out of nowhere, another shark came and smacked itself right into the tiger shark!

"Hammerhead!" Tammy screeched. She could recognize her odd-shaped shark friend anywhere.

Tammy bent down to Hammerhead and reached out. But she noticed that Hammerhead wasn't swimming toward her. And there was something red glistening in the ocean.

Hammerhead might have jumped in front of the tiger shark to save Leo, but she also got hurt in the process. Her dorsal fin was badly damaged.

"Oh no, no, no, *no*," Tammy screeched. Her friend was hurting. What was she going to do?

•

Hammerhead's vision was blurry. All she knew was that she'd jumped in front of Tiger and a kid. Tiger was prepared to bite, and Hammerhead could not let that happen.

Of course, Tiger was also a strong shark. His bite had injured her fin significantly. Hammerhead might have saved the kid, but her whole left side felt terrible.

Hammerhead! screeched Mako from beneath the sea. *You're hurt.*

Hammerhead wanted to bubble back a "yes," but she felt too much in pain. Instead, she squared her eyes on Tiger.

How could you do this? Hammerhead sounded. *We trusted you. We took you into our club!*

The kids were dangerous, Tiger replied. *They could have just as easily hurt you. That one reached out to me and it looked like he wanted to attack! I wanted to make sure they didn't bother us again.*

Hammerhead did not agree with Tiger, but at least she understood. Tiger really hadn't meant any harm. The kid had approached Tiger, not the other way around. It only made sense.

As Hammerhead started to drift in near-consciousness, she could feel a paddling at the top of the water. *What was that?* Hammerhead thought. She looked up and it was Tammy, trying to reach her.

I understand where you're coming from, what you've been led to believe, but these kids aren't dangerous, Tiger, Hammerhead motioned back. *They're trying to help. They're trying to be our friends. And now . . . now I need some help.*

Hammerhead closed her eyes. There was only one thing left to do.

As swiftly as possible, Hammerhead floated up. Right to Tammy, right to where the water met the sky.

Wow, thought Porbeagle.

His friend was flying.

•

When Hammerhead reached the top, Tammy dashed into the water. She didn't care how ridiculous she looked, or what Beckah and Carina and Leo might say, or whatever else happened. All Tammy knew was that her friend was in trouble. And she needed to help her.

Tammy cradled Hammerhead in her arms. Then she got an idea.

"Beckah," Tammy called out. "You're the only one here who has my grandfather's phone number. Can you call him, please? He'll know someone who can help."

At first it seemed like Beckah would give an excuse or protest, but then she looked at Tammy and the shark (it was quite a spectacle) and she nodded. She dialed Tammy's grandfather in Japan on her international app.

"Hi, Mr. Aiko? This is Beckah Cohen," she said, ever so calmly into the phone. "There's an emergency. And we need your help."

Tammy's grandfather promised to send over a marine animal rehabilitation specialist as soon as possible.

Hammerhead was in a dire place.

ELEVEN

Two Weeks Later

Two weeks later, Tammy and the Marine Science Club were back on the beach. Some of the other kids were there from school too. They were all gathered at Tiburon Cove, where something very special was happening. Beckah and Carina were there, cameras in hand. Leo McCormack was there with a video camera. And there were even some local news stations and radio stations.

"After spending fourteen days at the Waverly Marine Science Rehabilitation Center, we are pleased to return this female hammerhead shark to the ocean," said a marine biologist from the center. "She's good as new. And a pretty feisty shark, if I do say so myself!"

The marine biologist lowered a tank into the water. Inside was Hammerhead, who looked positively gleeful to be returning to the ocean. Hammerhead cast a glance around at everyone on the scene. There were certainly a lot of people to see her off!

Tammy flashed a smile at the hammerhead shark. She was so happy that her friend was okay. It had been scary when Hammerhead sacrificed herself for Leo, but Tammy was glad it had all worked out. The rehabilitation center used something called a prosthesis, or a fake fin, for Hammerhead, but she really looked just as she had before. They had even explained that it would feel the same for Hammerhead as it had before. And Hammerhead seemed to be in *great* spirits. She almost seemed to be waving at the crowd!

"Now, I'd love some help putting this shark back in the water," the biologist said. She motioned to the Marine Science Club. "Can the Waverly Middle School Marine Science Club assist me, please?"

Tammy, Alex, and Kyle smiled. Meanwhile, Beckah and Carina whooped.

"Yeah! You got this!" Beckah yelled, flashing her brilliantly white smile.

Tammy gave Hammerhead a pat on the head.

"I'm so glad you're okay," she told the shark.

While the biologist and the club members prepared Hammerhead to return to the ocean, a small, scrawny seagull was watching the spectacle unfold. And the seagull knew just what to do. It took off, soaring in the opposite direction—until it was out in the water, and looking down at the shadow of three sharks!

Squawk! the seagull called.

Mako, down at the bottom of the sea, looked up. Mako and Porbeagle had told the seagull to inform them when Hammerhead would be back. And now that they saw the seagull flying overhead . . . it seemed like their dear friend might return!

Everything's going to be okay! Porbeagle nearly screech-bubbled. *Seagull's got news for us. Mako, let's go! Scram, scram, scram!*

Mako was ready, but then he thought of someone else too. Someone who needed to see that humans weren't all that bad.

And for that, Mako went out and got Tiger, who had had a very rough two weeks.

•

Tiger didn't like to think of himself as a rough shark or a rogue shark. Tiger was simply protective of his friends. And when they went out and did things that Tiger didn't approve of . . . well, that's when the rocks hit the waters, or so the great white sharks liked to say!

Tiger hadn't meant to injure Hammerhead. Not at all! But that one tall kid had really thrown Tiger for a loop. Tiger thought he was *attacking* them. And Tiger was almost certain that when the humans had seen Hammerhead, she was done for. They hadn't heard anything in fourteen sleeps. But with the seagull's news, it seemed like Hammerhead would be back. Which meant . . . maybe humans weren't bad after all.

•

Beckah took a nice picture of Tammy for the paper. Then the MSC and the rehabilitation center scientists returned Hammerhead to the ocean, officially.

"And that's marine science for you," Tammy said, smiling to herself. She had felt so bad that the humans had taken Hammerhead away from her home for so long. But Hammerhead had communicated to her that she had always wanted to fly . . . and she finally got to do that!

Suddenly, there was a bubbling coming up from the water. It was three sharks! Mako, Porbeagle, and . . . could that be the tiger shark from before?

When the three sharks saw Hammerhead return, Tammy could almost see them breathe sighs of relief. They went to join their friend and kept nuzzling against her.

"That's amazing," breathed Leo, who was close enough for Tammy to hear.

It seemed the tiger shark heard Leo. Its interest was piqued. It swam over.

Oh no, Tammy thought. Last time, that didn't go over so well.

But instead of attacking, the tiger shark seemed to lift a fin up as if to say, "Hey." Leo was skeptical at first, but then he lifted a palm up to say "hey" too.

"Is that what he wants me to do?" Leo asked, facing Tammy.

"I'm not sure," Alex replied for her. "We've never seen tiger sharks behave like that before. This is totally uncharted territory, my man."

Leo looked at the tiger shark's protruding fin.

"Well, here goes nothing," he said, and drew a fresh breath. *"High fin!"*

Leo gave the tiger shark a high five. And the tiger shark gave one back!

"You know," Leo said, smiling at Tammy and the rest of the MSC. "I think I might be interested in joining your club. For real."

•

Marine Science Club Is Waverly Middle School's Next Big Thing

By Beckah Cohen

Photos by Carina Rodriguez

Seventh graders Tamera Aiko, Alexander de la Cruz, and Kyle Ray have something in common: They're the founding members of Waverly Middle School's inaugural Marine Science Club.

"I got the idea from my grandfather," said Aiko. "He's a marine biologist in Japan."

At the first meeting of the club, something miraculous happened—the trio befriended three wild sharks! Then they even saved one shark, a porbeagle, from certain doom. The porbeagle shark got caught in unrecycled plastic.

After this event, the Marine Science Club, also known as the MSC, was inspired to give back to the oceans.

They organized a school-wide beach cleanup field trip called "Marine Science Presents: Beach Day!"

More than forty students attended, each armed with a biodegradable plastic bag for picking up trash. The winner, sixth grader Allison Li, received a gift card to De La Cruz Pizzeria, the pizza shop on the boardwalk that de la Cruz's parents own.

At the beach field trip, the members also noticed a hammerhead shark who was in trouble. Thanks to Tammy's grandfather, they were able to connect with the Waverly Marine Science Rehabilitation Center and get the hammerhead shark back on its fins in no time.

"We're all very grateful to have been able to help this shark," said Ray, the club's treasurer. "And we hope to be back on the beach very soon."

The hammerhead was returned to the water this past Saturday. As for the club, it plans on having a new adventure ASAP.

"We're working on something. Something big, something bad, something that helps humankind and shark-kind alike. Stay tuned, folks, because it's going to be good," said the Marine Science Club's newest member, seventh grader Leonardo McCormack.

Tiger Shark

Tiger sharks are marine animals that mostly keep to themselves. They hunt at night. They eat a variety of food including: fish, seals, turtles, snakes, dolphins, birds, and crustaceans. They've also been known to eat smaller sharks.

Tiger sharks also have unique teeth. They poke out to the side in a sharp tip! This helps them eat food like turtle shells.

They're found mostly in tropical areas, including the Gulf of Mexico, Japan, and the Caribbean.